# Pug Blasts Off

# Read more Diary of a Pug books!

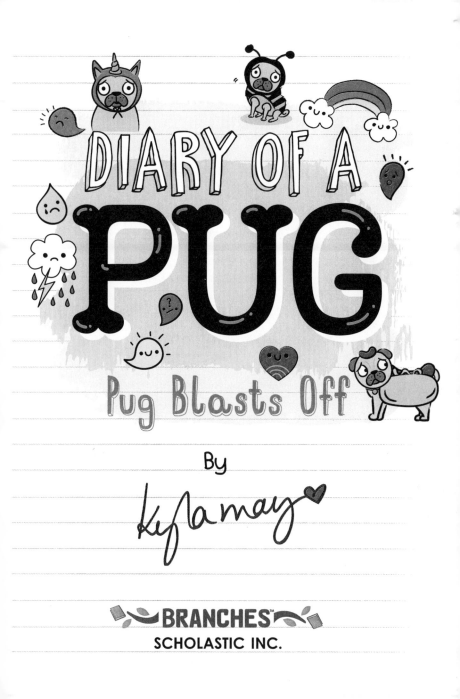

# DIARY OF A PUG

## Pug Blasts Off

By

*Kyla May*

BRANCHES™

SCHOLASTIC INC.

# To Mikka May

Special thanks to Sonia Sander

Art copyright © 2019 by Kyla May
Text copyright © 2019 by Scholastic Inc.

Photos © KylaMay2019

Library of Congress Cataloging-in-Publication Data

Names: May, Kyla, author, illustrator. Title: Pug Blasts Off / by Kyla May. Description: First edition. l New York, NY : Branches/Scholastic Inc., 2019. l Series: Diary of a pug ; [1] l Summary: Baron von Bubbles (Bub) is a pug who wants nothing more than to help his human Bella in her craft projects for school, though he is a little apprehensive about the rocket she is making for the Inventor Challenge—so when he ruins the rocket while trying to get at Nutz the squirrel he needs to find a way to make it up to Bella. Identifiers: LCCN 2019001963l ISBN 978-1-338-53003-2 (digest pbk.) l ISBN 978-1-338-53004-9 (reinforced library binding)
Subjects: LCSH: Pug—Juvenile fiction. l Human-animal relationships—Juvenile fiction. l Inventions—Juvenile fiction. l Squirrels—Juvenile fiction. l Diaries—Juvenile fiction. l Humorous stories. l CYAC: Pug—Fiction. l Dogs—Fiction. l Human-animal relationships—Fiction. l Inventions—Fiction. l Squirrels—Fiction. l Diaries—Fiction. l Humorous stories. l LCGFT: Humorous fiction. l Diary fiction.
Classification: LCC PZ7.M4535 Pu 2019 l DDC 813.6 [Fic] —dc23 LC record available at https://lccn.loc.gov/2019001963

10 9 8 7 6 5 4 3 2 1          19 20 21 22 23

Printed in China    62
First edition, October 2019
Edited by Katie Woehr
Book design by Kyla May and Sarah Dvojack

# Table of Contents



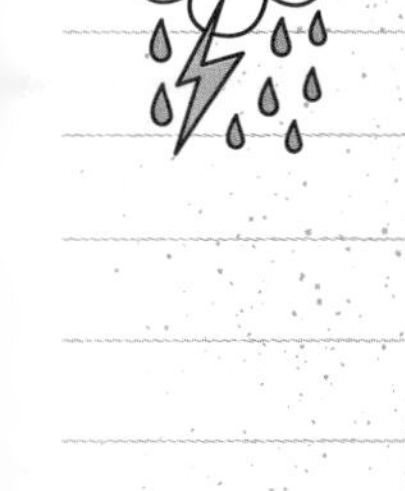

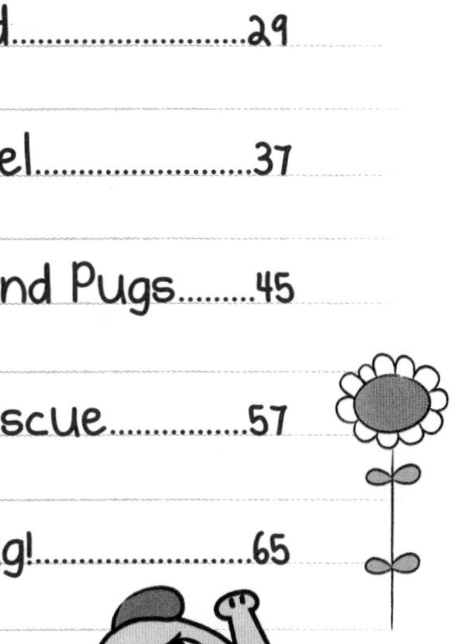

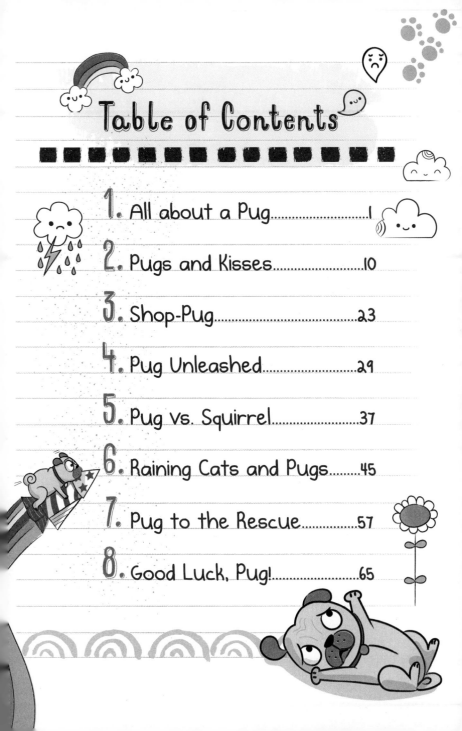

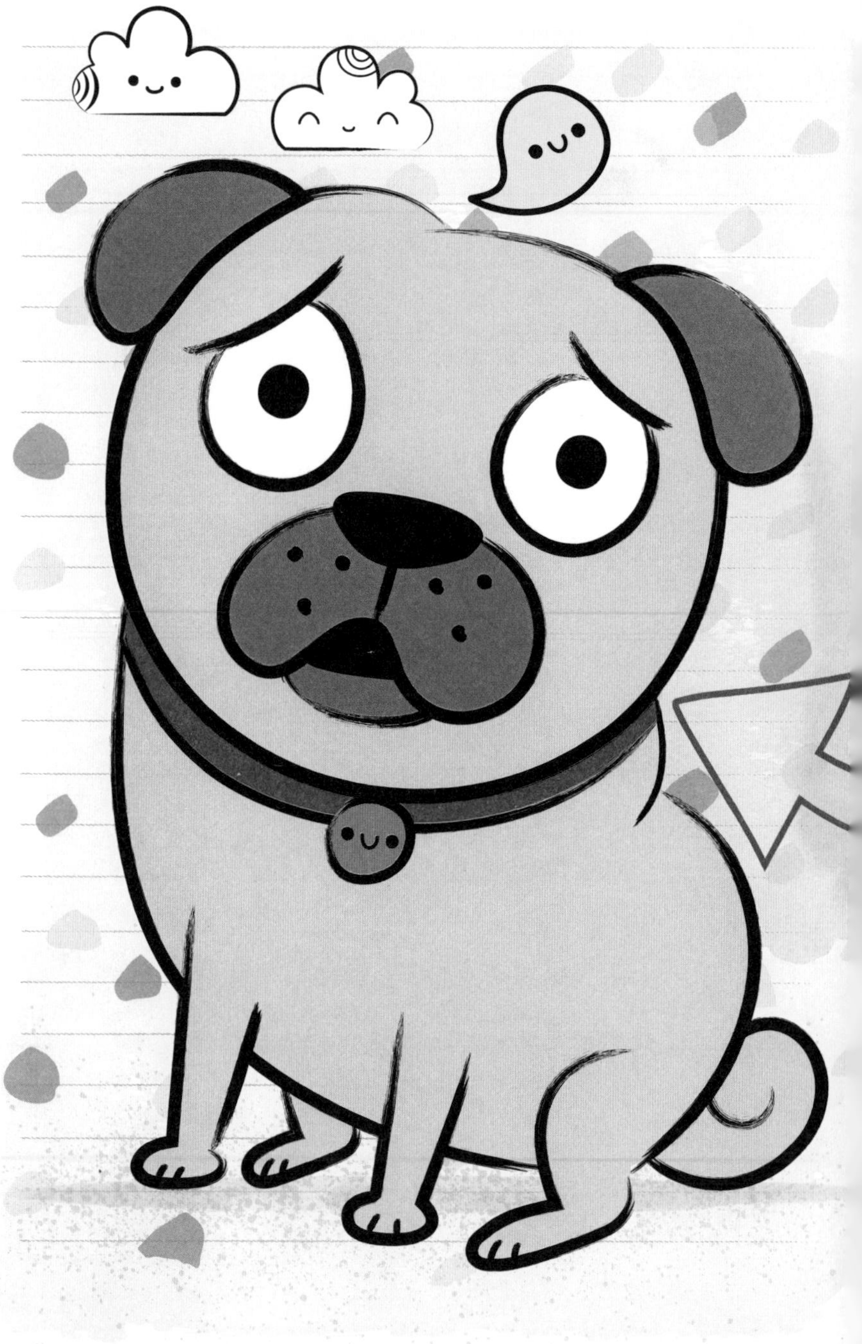

# Chapter 1

## ALL ABOUT A PUG

FRIDAY

Dear Diary,

BARON VON BUBBLES here. But everyone calls me

# BUB.

Here are some things to know about me:

I always dress to impress.

#pugunicorn

#pugbumblebee

#pughotdog

## I make many different faces:

Belly Rub Face

Have to Go Out Face

REALLY Have to
Go Out Face

Face for Duchess
(She acts like she owns the place.)

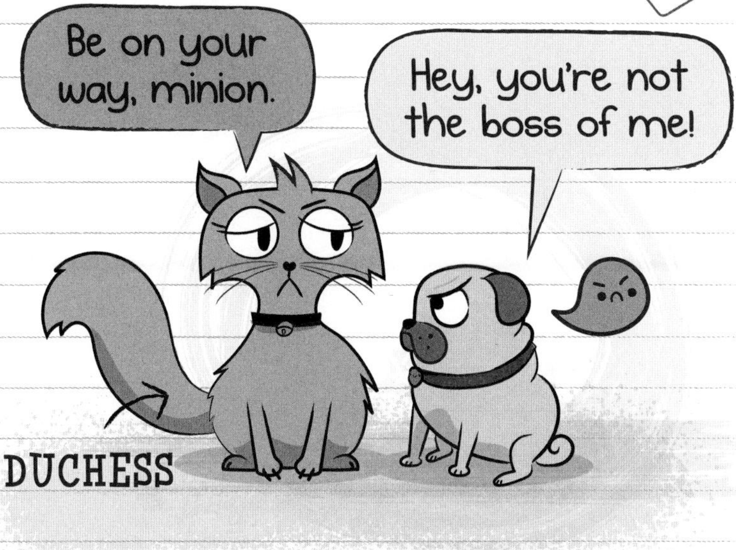
Be on your way, minion.
Hey, you're not the boss of me!
DUCHESS

Face for Nutz
(He steals my stuff all the time.)

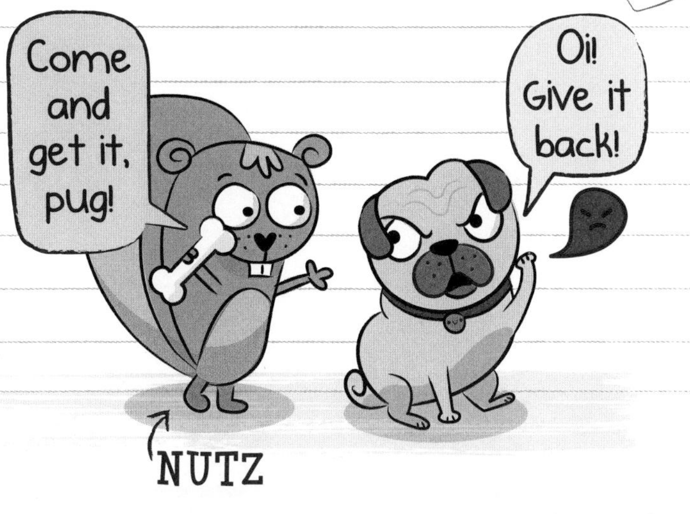
Come and get it, pug!
Oi! Give it back!
NUTZ

# Here are some of my favorite things:

MY SKATEBOARD

BEAR

PEANUT BUTTER

You know what is NOT my favorite?

GETTING WET.
When my human, Bella, first brought me home, I jumped into a bubble bath with her. But eeeek! There was WATER under the bubbles! Bella laughed so hard. (That's how I got my name, by the way.)

You know what else is wet? RAIN. I will NOT go out in the rain. Not even if I have to do my business.

No! NO!

No! NO! NO!

But back to Bella. She is the most important thing in my life. We met at a pet adoption fair. It was love at first sniff.

We have loads of fun together. One of our favorite things to do is ARTS AND CRAFTS.

But she can be forgetful sometimes, like when she forgets her lunch for school. I always help her out.

Thanks, Bub!

Speaking of school, I miss Bella so much when she is there.

But woo-hoo! It's Friday today. It's the weekend! I get two whole days with Bella! I gave her the best welcome home this afternoon.

Guess what? I have a surprise for you! But...

...it will have to wait until tomorrow. I'm too tired to show it to you now. Let's just snuggle, okay?

Diary—I love snuggling, but I can't stop thinking about the surprise. What could it be?

# Chapter 2

🐶 X 🐶 X

## PUGS AND KISSES

### SATURDAY

Dear Diary,

This morning, I HAD to find out what the surprise was, so I tried to wake Bella up super early.

ATTEMPT #1:

LICK LICK

That tickles, Bubby.

ATTEMPT #2:

I thought Sleeping Beauty would NEVER get up. I finally used my no-fail move.

## ATTEMPT #3:

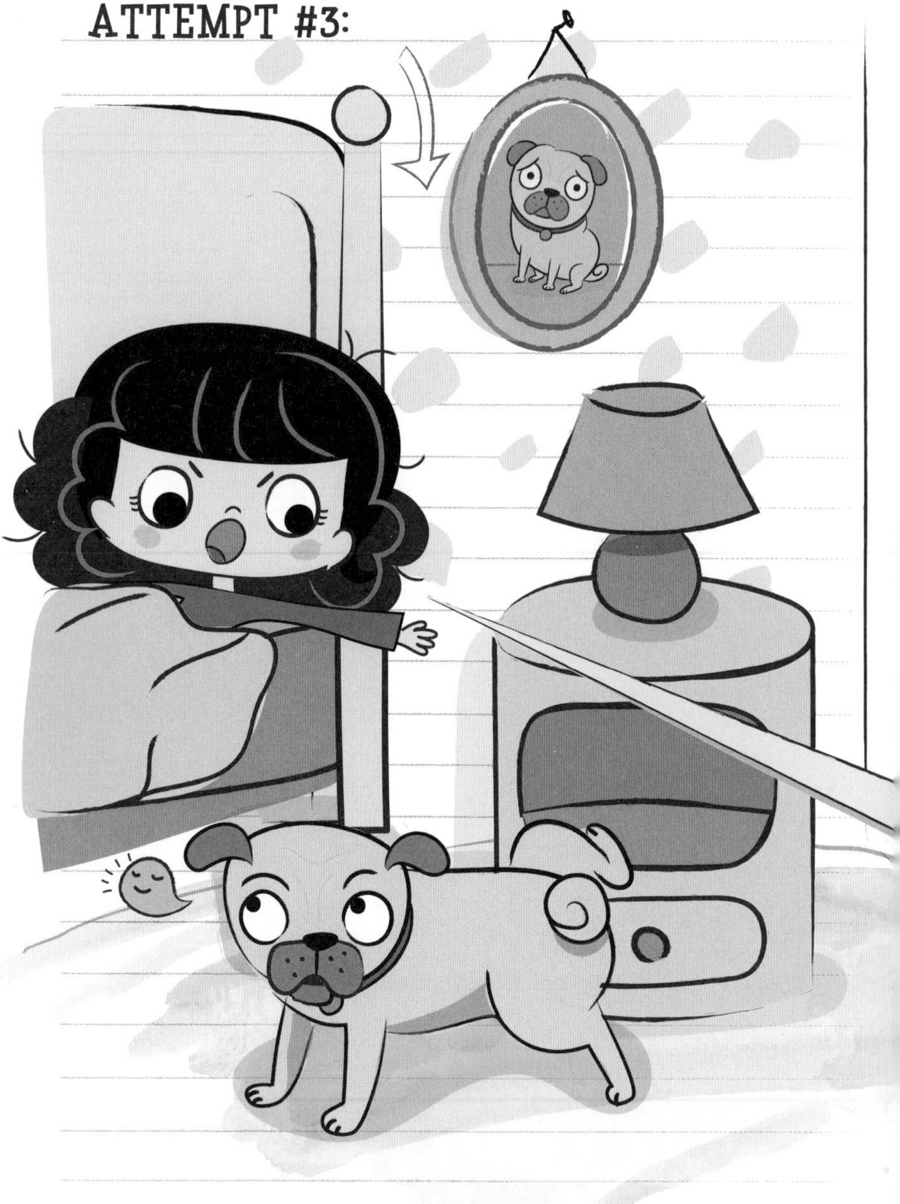

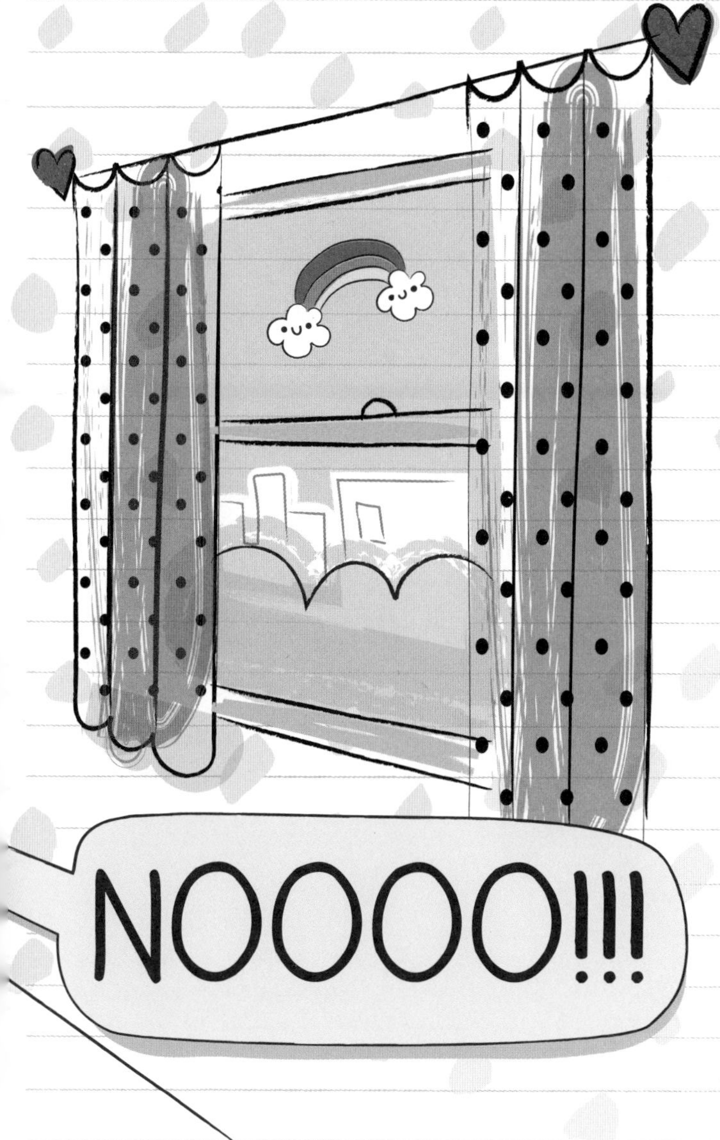
NOOOO!!!

Haha! She falls for that every time!

So now that you're up...

Okay, okay! I'll show you the surprise. Ready?

Inventor Challenge!

Show off your creativity by crafting your own invention!

Prizes for Best Invention, Most Creative Invention, and more!

When? This Friday!

Oh boy! An arts-and-crafts project to do together! I had so many ideas already.

But Bella wanted to do some research first. It went very, veeeeerrrrry slowly. I tried my best to help.

We just need to find the right project.

Do you mind, Duchess?

Not at all, Bubby-kins.

Oh, Diary—I hate it so much when Duchess calls me that. I couldn't let her get away with it!

I chased her through
the kitchen . . .

And the living room . . .

And finally back to Bella's room.

I had almost caught her when—

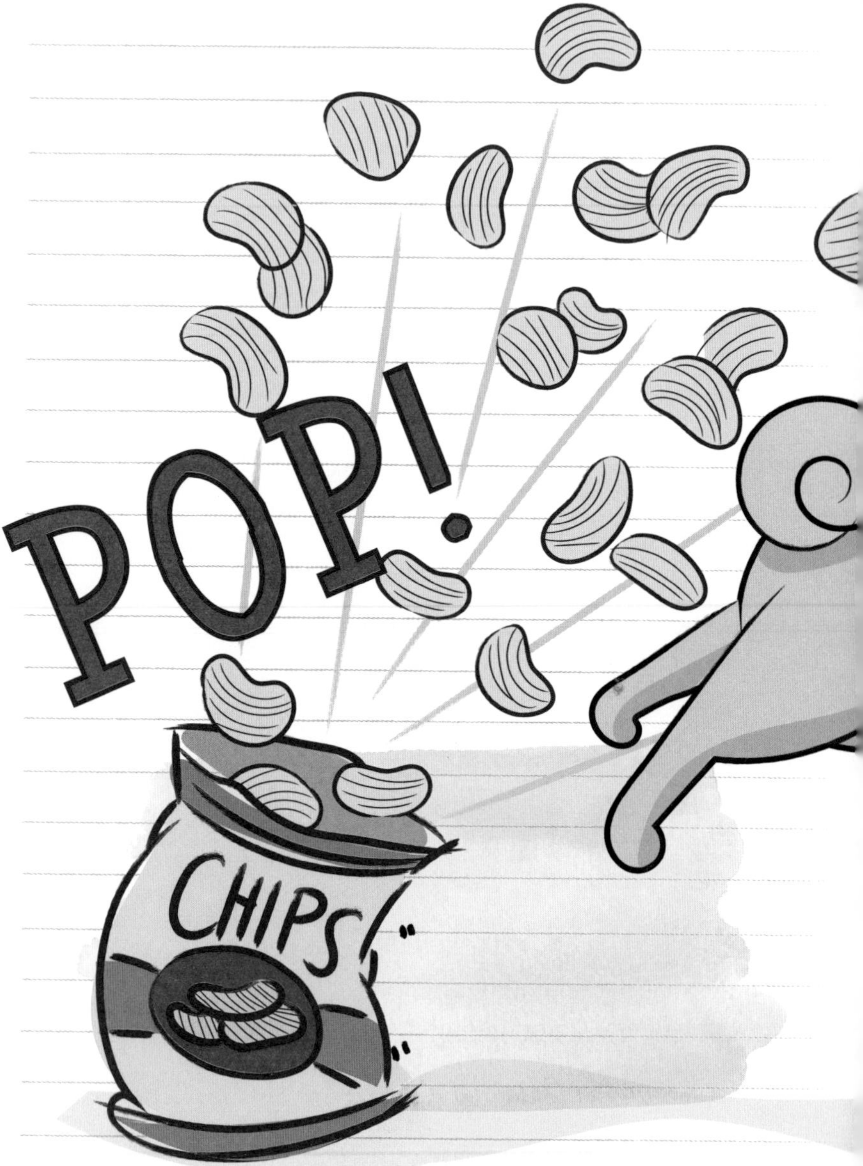
POP!
CHIPS

I would have had a good
comeback, I swear. But
I was pretty HUNGRY.

Just then, Bella jumped to her feet.

Those exploding chips gave me an awesome idea, Bubby! I know what we'll do for the invention. But we need supplies. Let's go shopping tomorrow!

I had no clue what her idea was, Diary. But I never pass up an excuse to shop. Not ever!

# Chapter 3

## SHOP-PUG

SUNDAY

Dear Diary,

Before we hit the shops, Bella and I tried on a million outfits until we found just the right ones.

Ta-daaaaa!

Who wore it better?

At the craft store, I tried to guess what the invention could be.

**CARDBOARD**
Oh no. Duchess loves cardboard. This project better not be something for her. That would be the worst.

**TAPE**
That's not much better. Last time I used tape, it did NOT go well.

By the time we paid for the supplies, I still had **NO CLUE** what the invention would be. But Diary, as we headed home, my **WORST NIGHTMARE** came true. It began to rain! I had to get creative to stay dry.

Silly pug! It's just a little water.

To you, maybe. To me, it's **THE ENEMY.**

I was so happy when we were home and dry!

As Bella got to work on the mystery invention, I was the best assistant ever.

But I **KNEW** that tape was trouble.

Oops!

Finally, Bella added one last piece to the invention. All of a sudden, I knew what it was!

A rocket! This was going to win the **INVENTOR CHALLENGE** for sure! I showed Bella how proud of her I was.

LICK LICK

I have until Friday to make sure the invention is perfect. You and I can test it outside tomorrow after school, okay? We'll be flying high in no time, Bub!

Wait. **WHAT?!** Did Bella think I was going to **FLY** in the rocket? Oh no, Diary. I have a bad feeling about this . . .

# Chapter 4

# PUG UNLEASHED

## MONDAY

Dear Diary,

Bella left for school this morning. I worried about flying in that rocket all day long. Imagine me, an astronaut! I was totally off my game. I didn't even feel like annoying Duchess.

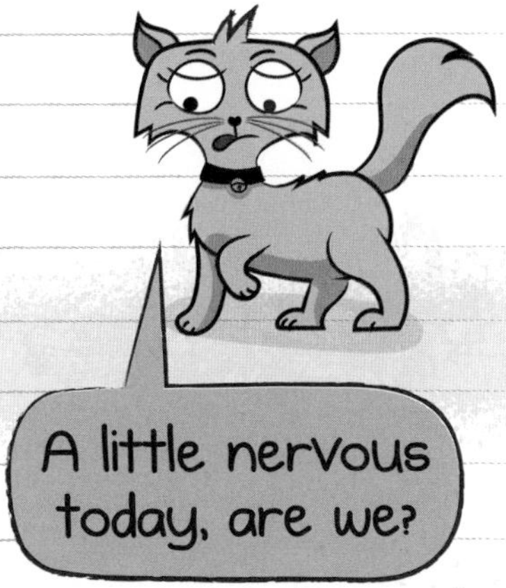
A little nervous today, are we?

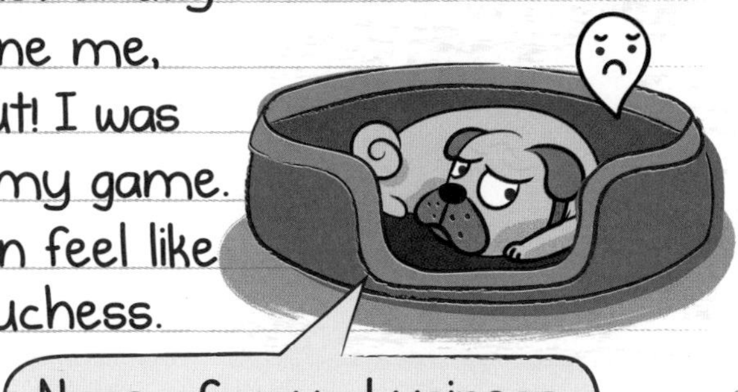
None of your business.

Usually, it seems like forever until Bella comes home. But today, the hours flew by. I did NOT want to go in that rocket, no sir. At my lowest moment, I even hoped it would rain. Then we would not be able to test the rocket outside. Can you imagine, Diary? Baron von Bubbles actually WANTING it to rain!

Before I knew it, Bella was home. I tried to give her a nice welcome, but my tail couldn't even wag.

Bella took the rocket out to the yard.
I brought Bear with me for good luck.

It's almost time for blast off!
Stand back, Bub!

Huh?
Stand back?!

It turned out Bella never wanted me
to fly the rocket. Phew! I went to grab
Bear to celebrate, but Bear was not
there. Just then, a gray streak dashed
across the yard!

Oh, that Nutz! He is the sneakiest squirrel around. I had to rescue Bear. But Nutz ran up the tree to where I could not reach him. (These legs are NOT designed to climb.)

Bella was counting down to the rocket blastoff.

Suddenly, it hit me: The rocket would be the perfect ride up to Nutz! I was nervous, Diary, but Bear needed me.

At the last second, I jumped on the rocket and BLASTED OFF.

**AAAAAAAAHHHH!**
The rocket flipped and
spun out of control. I made
it to the tree, alright.

# SPLAT!

Oh, Bubby, are you okay?

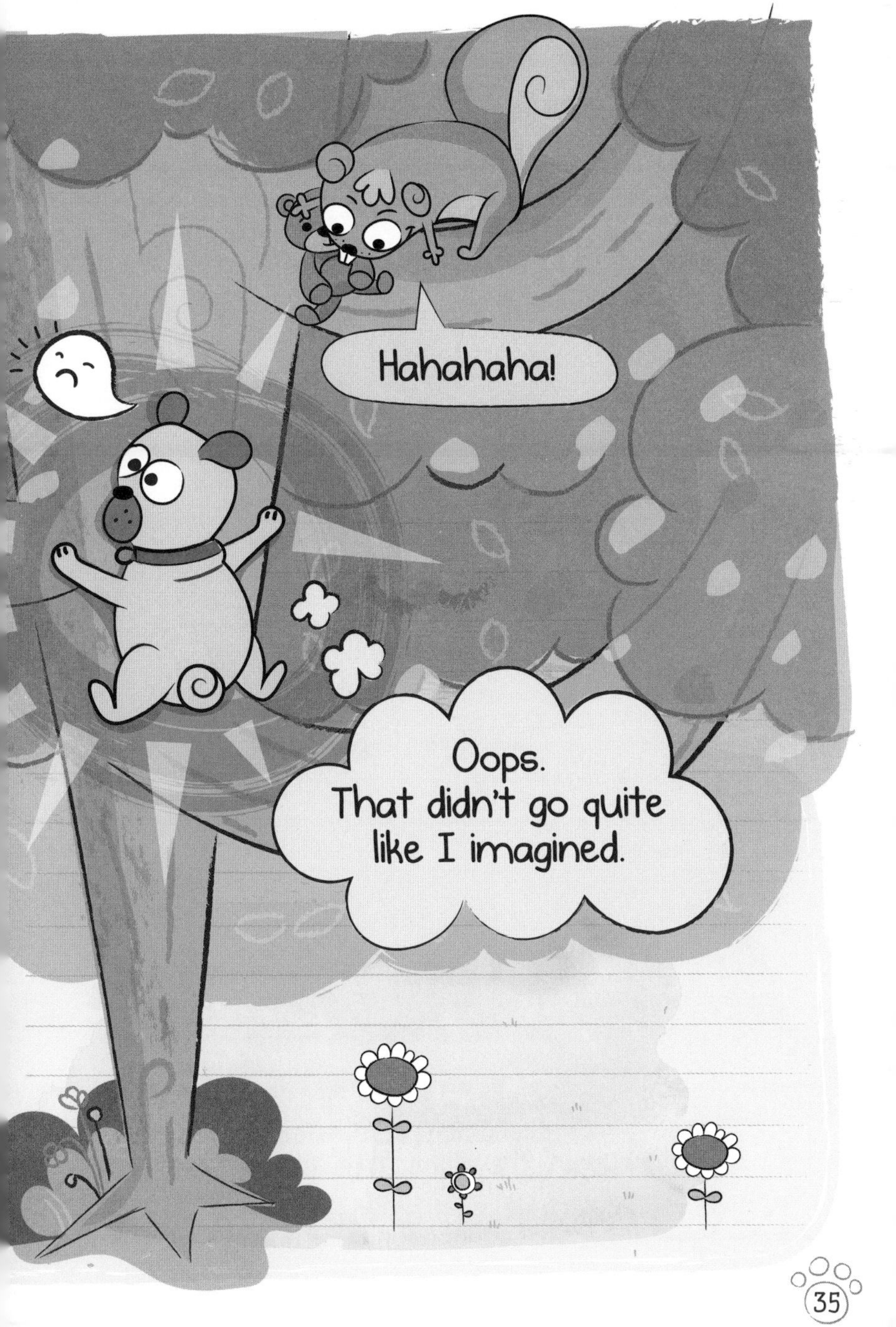
Hahahaha!
Oops.
That didn't go quite
like I imagined.

Bella got me down, but I've never seen her so sad. The rocket was in pieces all over the yard. We gathered some parts of it, but others are still missing. It's all my fault.

Oh, Bub, we are never going to win now.

Diary, I can't stand seeing Bella so sad. I didn't mean to ruin the invention. I have to make it up to her. But how?

# Chapter 5

## PUG VS. SQUIRREL

TUESDAY

Dear Diary,

I spent all morning searching for the missing rocket pieces.

SNIFF SNIFF

I found almost all of them. I found Bear, too. But there was one piece still missing—a wing. Guess who had it?

I used my famous BEGGING FACE on Nutz.

Please, please, please, please, please give it back?

But Nutz wanted to make a deal.

If I give you the wing, what will you give me in exchange?

I racked my brain—what could I trade with Nutz?

Hmmm... What does Nutz love? He loves to annoy me...

Wait! Nutz LOVES peanuts! I bet Nutz would REALLY LOVE peanut butter!

I was not exactly thrilled to give up some peanut butter, but I had no choice. Anything to make Bella happy again.

Nutz had never heard of peanut butter before, so I had to really talk it up. This required a special outfit, of course.

I could tell Nutz was interested. His tail was twitching. Finally, he ran down the tree trunk.

I couldn't believe it! But, oops. I had only ONE jar of peanut butter with me, so I raced back inside to get another.

I grabbed a second jar from the pantry and dashed back outside just as—

BOOM! The sky clapped with thunder. Rain came pouring down.

Diary, I had no choice. The deal would have to wait until tomorrow.

Bella came home from school a little later. I tried to tell her about my day. I showed her all the rocket parts I found.

You're a good dog, Bub. But we're still missing the wing. The most important part.

Bella searched for the wing herself, but Nutz must have hidden it. She tried to make a new wing, but we didn't have enough cardboard (or tape).

I have made a promise to myself, Diary. Rain or no rain, I <u>will</u> get that wing for Bella tomorrow!

# Chapter 6

## RAINING CATS AND PUGS

**WEDNESDAY**

Dear Diary,

There are only TWO more days until the Inventor Challenge! Today was my last chance to make this right. But it was raining again, so I had to think creatively.

Maybe I could use a catapult to launch the peanut butter to Nutz.

CATAPULT

Maybe I could send the peanut butter to Nutz on Bella's old fire truck.

Or not.

**NEW PLAN:** I would go out in the rain. But I would NOT get wet!

The bucket seemed like a good idea at first.

My **SECOND IDEA** seemed promising . . . until I went outside.

Back inside, I sat down to problem solve. There **HAD** to be a way to get the peanut butter to Nutz <u>without</u> getting rained on.

Need some help, Bubby-kins?

Shhhhh... I'm thinking. Hey—wait a minute!

I had the best idea in the history of ideas, Diary. I would build a tunnel to the tree!

I grabbed as many waterproof things as I could find. I set them up to cover my path to the tree.

Bella arrived home from school just as I decided to go for it.

Here goes nothing!

PLASTIC WRAP

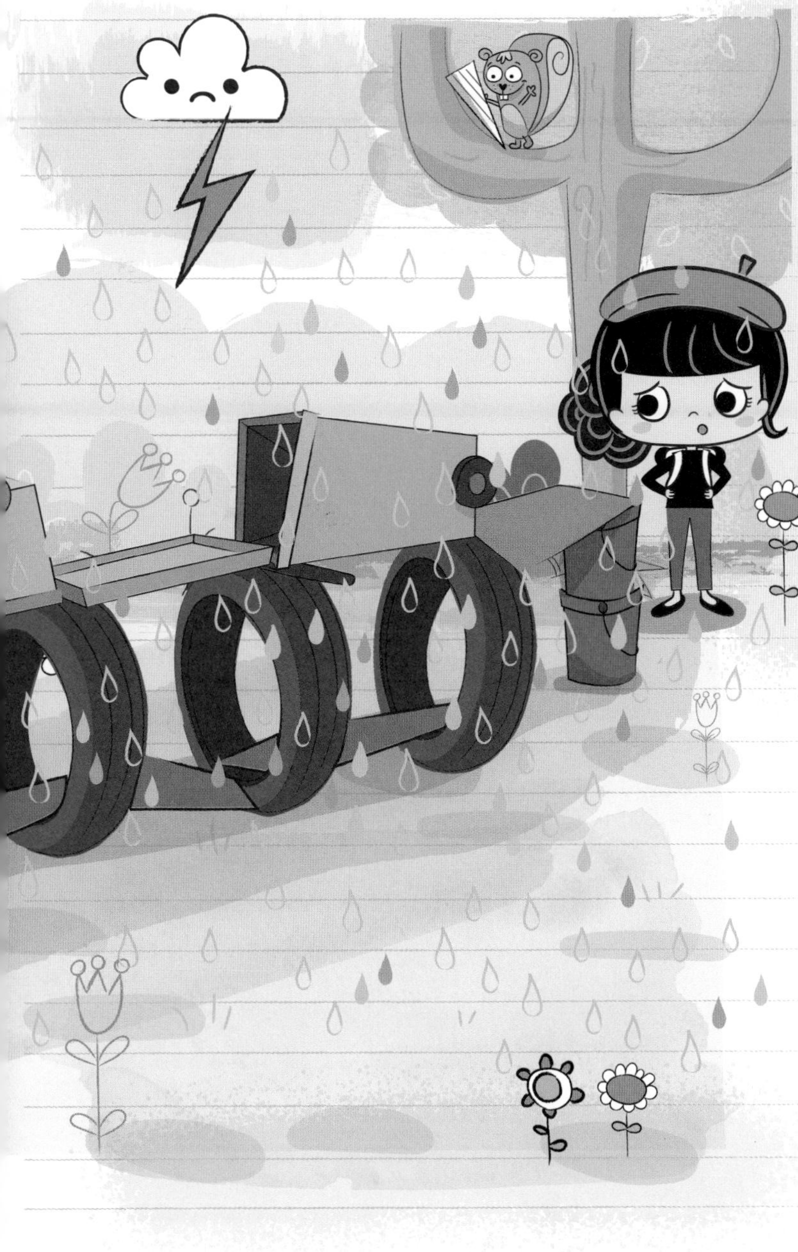

The first part of the tunnel was solid, but halfway to the tree I slipped on some mud. The peanut butter went flying. Everything is a big blur after that.

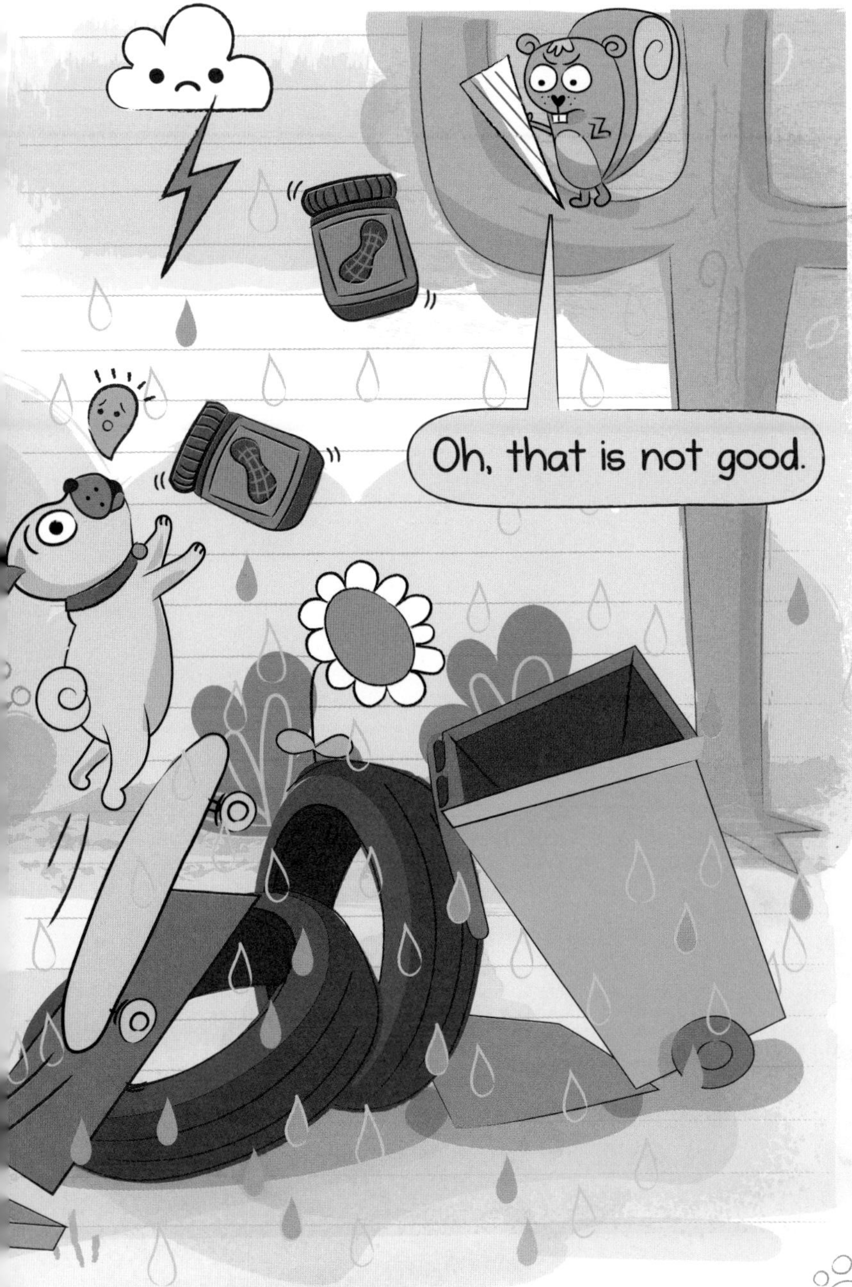
Oh, that is not good.

I was still dizzy—and very wet—when Bella saved me. But guess what, Diary? Nutz GAVE UP THE WING!

My brave, Bubby!! You found the wing AND you went out in the rain for me! I love you so much. You are the best dog ever!

I was SO tired, I didn't even mind the bath Bella gave me after that. But Diary, the weirdest thing happened!

Look, Bub! Even Duchess is impressed with what you did today.

Not bad, pug. Not bad.

Huh?! Did Duchess just say something NICE to me?!

As Bella tucked me in, she whispered to me.

We have all the rocket parts now, Bub. But your work today gave me an idea for an EVEN BETTER invention! We can build it tomorrow after school, okay?

Another invention?! Diary, I am waaaay too tired to think about another project now. Good night!

## Chapter 7

# PUG TO THE RESCUE

**THURSDAY**

Dear Diary,

We had lots to do today. Bella's new idea is fantastic. Mostly because it's starring ME! The cutest pug on the planet.

Bella wanted to build a rain shelter for me. I will never have to do my business in the rain ever again. WOO-HOO!

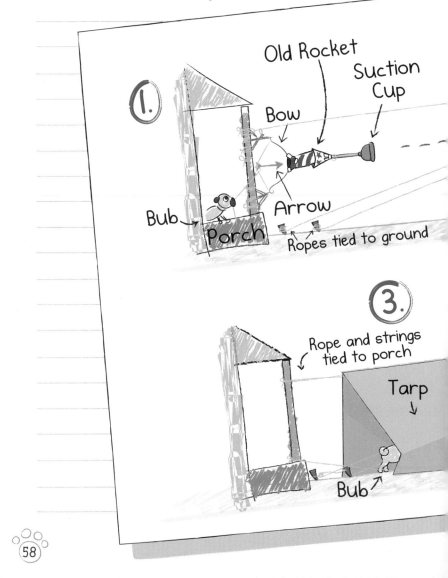

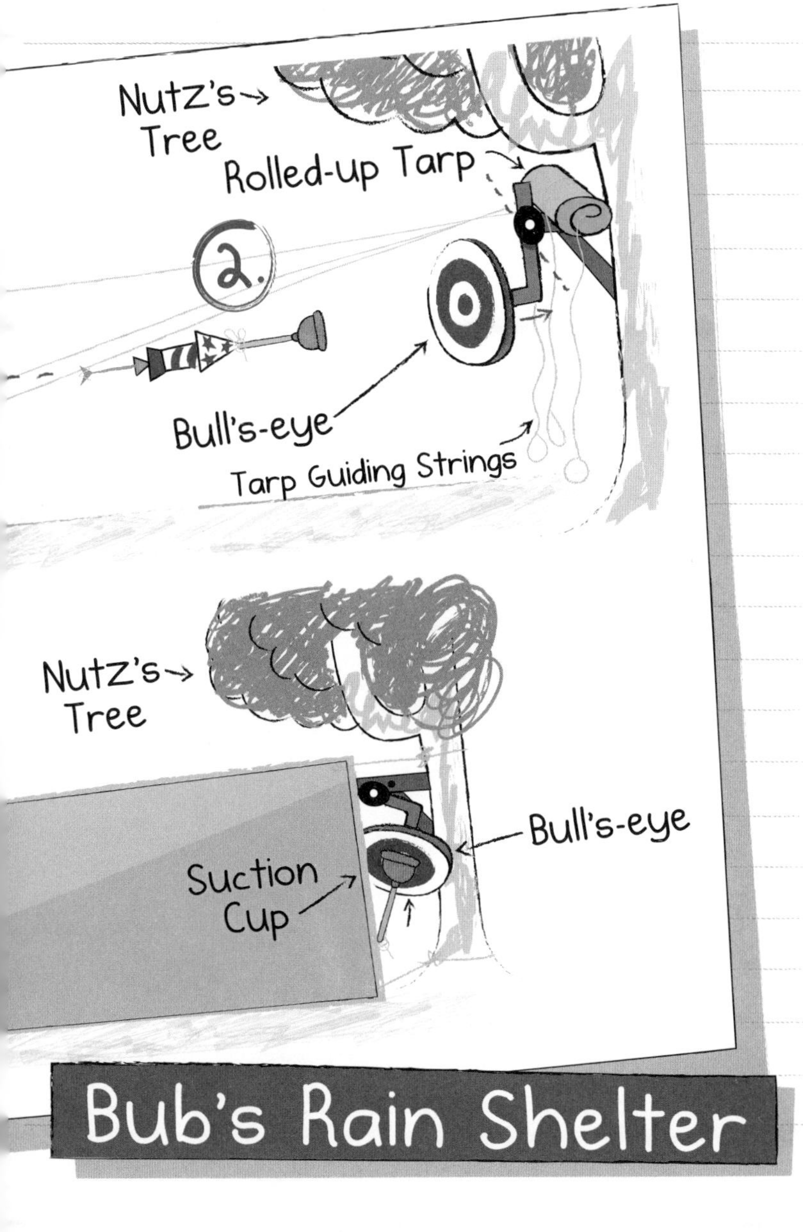
Nutz's Tree
Rolled-up Tarp
2.
Bull's-eye
Tarp Guiding Strings
Nutz's Tree
Bull's-eye
Suction Cup

# Bub's Rain Shelter

The sun was out today—phew! We built my shelter in the yard. I was a big help.

We worked from three o'clock until sundown. We didn't even stop for dinner. Finally, the shelter was ready.

This was the moment of truth. I grabbed the rope. Then I tugged as hard as I could.

The rocket flew through the air. It triggered the latch on the tarp. The tarp unrolled and fell right into place.

Bella and I packed the project up to take to the **INVENTOR'S CHALLENGE** tomorrow. Then we tried to get some sleep. But I couldn't help wondering, Diary. The shelter machine worked here . . . Would it work at school?

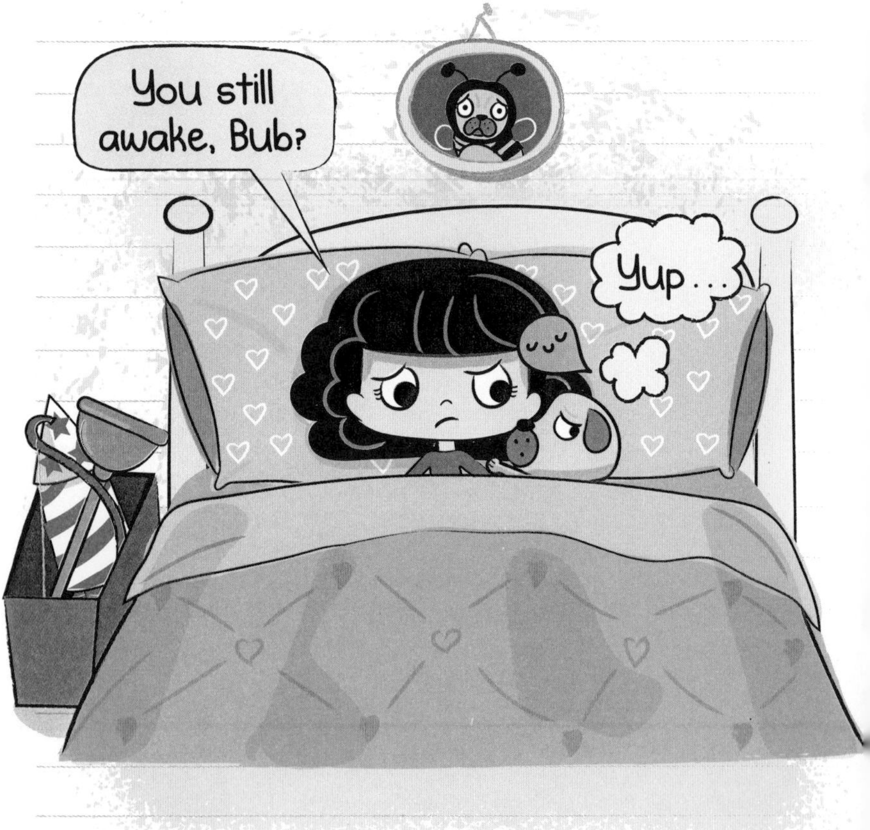
You still awake, Bub?
Yup . . .

# Chapter 8

## GOOD LUCK, PUG!

FRIDAY

Dear Diary,

I was sooooo nervous this morning. And, oops! Sometimes things…happen…when I'm nervous.

Ew, yuck!

Poor, Bubby! Don't worry. Let's get dressed… What should we wear?

FASHION—the perfect thing to take my mind off my nerves!

We found just the right outfits, then headed to school.

I made sure nothing was left behind.

Don't forget this!

What would I do without you, Bub?

Duchess dashed out of the house before we left and handed me the bell from her collar.

It's my good luck charm. You can borrow it today.

Wow! Thanks, Duchess!

It's not a big deal. Don't get all mushy.

I can't believe I'm saying this, Diary, but maybe Duchess isn't that bad?

We set up the machine in Bella's school gym. There were so many other cool projects! I got nervous all over again.

Oh, Bubby. Are you feeling sick again? It's okay. You are going to do great!

Inventor Challeng

Sorry!

Oops...sorry again.

Before long, it was time
for our big moment!
Would the machine
work at school just like
it did at home? I pulled
on the rope...

And it worked! YIPPEEEEE! I forgot about my nerves. Everything went perfectly!

Can you believe it, Diary?

We won **BEST PET INVENTION!**

I couldn't have done it without you, Bub!

We make a great team!

Back at home, Bella had another surprise for me.

My new rain coat is super-duper
awesome, Diary. Bella is, too.

## About the Creator

Kyla May is an Australian illustrator, writer, and designer. In addition to books, Kyla creates animation. She lives by the beach in Victoria, Australia, with her three daughters and her daughter's pug called Bear.

# HOW MUCH DO YOU KNOW ABOUT
# DIARY OF A PUG

## Pug Blasts Off?

A nickname is a short version of someone's name. Bella named me Baron von Bubbles, or "Bub" for short. Why?

How does Bub's brave attempt to rescue me from the tree go wrong?

What does Bub give me in order to get back Bella's rocket wing?

What problem did I solve for Bub with my winning invention?

Imagine you are entering an Inventor Challenge. First, write about what you would invent. Then draw a picture of your creation!

scholastic.com/branches